Nightmare Hour
Too Scared to Sleep

Nighttime:
Too Scared to Sleep

by Todd Strasser

Scholastic Inc.

New York   Toronto   London   Auckland   Sydney
Mexico City   New Delhi   Hong Kong   Buenos Aires

To Elena's daughter, Melanie
—T.S.

ISBN-13: 978-0-439-80067-9
ISBN-10: 0-439-80067-6

12 11 10 9 8 7 6 5 4 3   7 8 9 10 11 12/0

Printed in the U.S.A.
First printing, October 2007

CONTENTS

Whispers in the Dark

"You have to share your room with Megan," Mrs. Pickler said. She was holding the new baby in her arms. The baby's name was Peter. Megan was Billy Pickler's little sister.

"No!" Billy said. He crossed his arms and buried his chin against his chest.

"You'll only have to share for a few months," said his mother. "Just until we move to our new house."

"No!" Billy yelled.

"Billy, that's very selfish of you," scolded Mr. Pickler. "Megan's room is going to be the nursery for Peter. She has to move out. You get to keep your room. She can stay with you for a few months. I expect you to act like a big boy and help us with this."

Billy didn't want to help. The new baby was a big pain. All Peter did was cry. Everybody made a big fuss about him. And Megan was annoying. Billy didn't want her moving into his room. Mrs. Pickler whispered something to her husband.

"Come on, Billy," Mr. Pickler said. "Let's go play catch."

Billy and his father went to the park. Then Mr. Pickler bought him an ice cream. But when Mr. Pickler brought Billy home, there was an extra bed in Billy's bedroom. Megan was putting her dolls on the shelf above it.

"No!" Billy yelled. "I don't want those dolls in my room!"

"I need my dolls!" Megan cried.

"Not in my room!" Billy shouted.

Both kids started to scream. Finally, Mr. and

Mrs. Pickler made a decision. Megan would have one half of the room. Billy would have the other half. Megan would be allowed to keep two dolls on her shelf. She chose Jade and Cloe.

Billy refused to go into his room for the rest of the day. He hated dolls more than anything in the world.

That night, Megan went to bed at eight P.M. She was sound asleep when Billy's parents told him he had to go to bed. Billy went to his room. He was still angry that he had to share his room with his sister. And he was *very* angry that she had put her dolls on the shelf. He was so angry that he couldn't fall asleep.

Billy decided to sit in bed and read. He opened his favorite book, *The Scariest Stories Ever.* But when Billy started to read, he felt something strange. It felt as if he and his sister weren't the only ones in the room. Billy imagined that the dolls on the shelf were staring at him. They looked like they wanted to laugh because they got to be in his room and there was nothing Billy could do about it.

That just made Billy angrier. He decided to put

his two favorite wrestling action figures on the shelf across from the dolls. He made sure they were staring back. Then he fell asleep.

The next afternoon, Megan had a playdate at a friend's house. Billy sat on the floor in his room playing with his wrestlers. But he could feel the eyes of his sister's dolls on him. He hated those dolls. And so did his wrestlers.

Billy had an idea. His parents had said he wasn't allowed to go into his sister's half of the room. But they'd said nothing about his action figures. With one wrestler in each hand, Billy reached across and took the blonde Cloe doll from the shelf.

Billy let his wrestlers twist the doll's head around. They stomped on Cloe's legs and body-slammed her to the ground. Billy felt happy. Those dolls were getting what they deserved. Then Billy heard the door open and close downstairs. He quickly put Cloe back on her shelf. Soon Megan came into the room. But she had no idea what had happened.

That night, Billy felt happy when he went to bed. His wrestlers had taught those dolls a lesson.

They wouldn't laugh at him again. He turned off the light and closed his eyes and started to fall asleep.

"Psssst!" Billy thought he heard something. It sounded like an angry whisper. Very softly, a girl's voice said, "You shouldn't have done that."

Billy opened his eyes. He sat up in bed and turned on the light. He quickly looked around, but he didn't see anyone else in the room. Megan was in her bed, sleeping soundly. Her dolls sat on the shelf. *Wait a minute!* Was it Billy's imagination, or did they look like they were frowning?

No, it couldn't be. Billy turned off the light and went to sleep.

The next afternoon, Mrs. Pickler took Megan to her skating lesson. Once again Billy played with his wrestlers in his room. This time, he had them take the dark-haired Jade doll from the shelf. Billy made the wrestlers twist her arms and legs. They put her in a sleeper hold. Just before Megan got home, he put the Jade doll back on the shelf.

That night, Megan went to bed at eight o'clock

again. When Billy went to bed, he turned off the light and snuggled under his blanket. He was almost asleep when he heard a girl whisper, "I've had enough of this."

And another voice angrily agreed. "It's time to put a stop to it."

Billy sat up and turned on the lights. This time, he was certain he'd heard a voice. His heart began to beat hard. He had to stop himself from running into his parents' bedroom. Nothing in the room looked different. Megan was in her bed, sleeping soundly. Billy wondered if he had imagined the whispers. Maybe it was a dream. The dolls sat on the shelf facing him. Did they look angry? Billy rolled over and turned his back to them. He tried to go back to sleep.

That night, Billy had a strange dream. There were tiny footsteps and the sounds of girls whispering. He dreamed he heard light scratching and soft grunts. Two small figures moved in the shadows.

In the morning, Billy and Megan got dressed. Megan went downstairs for breakfast. Billy started to follow. Then he remembered a book he needed for school. He went back to the bedroom. As he reached for the book, he glanced at his wrestlers.

Their hands were tied behind their backs.

Billy looked at Cloe and Jade on his sister's shelf.

He was certain they were smiling.

Halloween Music

"Andy!" yelled Michael.

"Hey, Andy!" called Zach.

"Earth to Andy!" said Garrett.

Andy Stone walked away down the sidewalk. He and his friends were carrying pillowcases. It was Halloween and they were trick-or-treating. But Andy's pillowcase was only half as full as the others'. His friends stood in a driveway and watched him walk away.

"Why does he keep wandering off?" Zach asked.

"Because he's listening to his iPod," Garrett said. "He always turns it up too loud. He must be the only kid in the world who likes music more than candy."

Andy kept walking. A thin white wire rose from his iPod to the small white earbuds in his ears.

"It's your turn to get him," Michael said to Zach.

"No way," said Zach. "I got him last time. It's Garrett's turn."

"OK," said Garrett, "but this is the last time. Next time he wanders off, I say we let him go."

Garrett went to get Andy, and the four boys continued trick-or-treating. But a few houses later, Andy wandered off again.

"That's it," Garrett muttered. "I'm tired of running after him. He's got to learn to pay attention."

"I've got an idea," whispered Zach.

A little while later, all four boys walked down a dark, shadowy street. A lone streetlight flickered. Only one house stood on this block. It was big and empty. The Marbury family had once lived there. But that was many years ago. The rusty gate creaked loudly when Michael pushed it open. The four boys went up the walk. They crossed the rotten old porch and pushed open the squeaky old door. Inside, the house was dark and smelled musty. Cobwebs hung in the doorways.

Andy stopped in the front hall and turned down the volume on his iPod. "What are we doing in here?" he asked.

"There's supposed to be a big barrel of candy hidden somewhere in this house," said Zach.

"But no one lives here," Andy said.

"Right," said Michael. "That's why they hid the barrel here."

That sounded strange to Andy. But he didn't really care. It was OK if his friends wanted to look for some mysterious barrel. He turned up the volume on his iPod and went with them.

"Let's make sure we stick together," said Zach.

The boys pretended to search the first floor. Then they headed upstairs. Sure enough, Andy wandered off down a hall, listening to his music.

"OK, guys," Zach whispered to Michael and Garrett. "Let's go outside and see what happens."

Andy listened to his iPod and strolled down a dark hallway inside the house. The air was chilly. Many of the windows were cracked or broken. Everything was old and dusty. Drafts made the cobwebs move. Most of the rooms were empty. Here and there, a table or chair was covered by an old white sheet.

To Andy, the whole place was just plain creepy. He got to the end of the hall and looked around. He doubted there was a barrel of candy in the house. And where were Zach, Garrett, and Michael, anyway?

"Guys?" Andy pulled the earbuds from his ears. "Hey, guys?"

No one answered. Suddenly, Andy knew he was alone. He felt a chill and his pulse began to race. The house was big and dark and scary. He wasn't sure he could find his way out. He walked back down the hall and called nervously. "Guys? *Guys!?*"

"Who's yelling?" a woman's voice asked.

Andy stopped and looked in the room the voice had come from. A beautiful young woman sat in a chair, lit by moonlight coming through a window. Her long red hair fell down over the shoulders of her long white dress. The moonlight made her glow.

"Who are you?" she asked.

"I'm Andy Stone. Who are you?"

"I'm Marjory Marbury," the woman said. "Did you come to visit?"

"Well, uh, I'm looking for my friends. They came here looking for candy."

Marjory Marbury blinked and sat up. "My goodness, you're right! It's Halloween."

"You didn't know that?" Andy asked.

"Forgive me," said the beautiful woman. "I always forget. Please help yourself." She pointed at a bowl on the table beside her. "And thank you for coming. I haven't had a visitor in so long."

Andy stepped closer and looked in the bowl. He frowned. He'd never seen candy like this before. "What is that?"

"Sweets, of course," said Marjory Marbury. "This

is rock candy, and this is licorice, and these are taffy. Please try some."

Marjory Marbury may have looked young, but she spoke the way people did in old black-and-white movies. Andy tried what she handed to him. The rock candy tasted sweet, like sugar. The licorice was strong, almost like cough syrup. When he put the taffy in his mouth, it felt hard. But soon it became chewy. "Can I take some to show my friends?" Andy asked. "I bet they've never seen candy like this."

"Certainly, you may," said Marjory. She looked at Andy and frowned. "What is that thing around your neck?"

"It's an iPod," Andy said.

"What does it do?" asked the woman.

Andy thought it was strange that she didn't know what an iPod was. But it was also strange that she was sitting in a dark room wearing a long white dress. And it was strange that she had offered him this odd candy. Andy took the earbuds from around his neck. "Put one in each ear."

Marjory Marbury did as he said. Andy picked

a song and played it for her. The woman's eyes widened with surprise. Then she gasped, "How marvelous!"

Andy's friends waited on the dark sidewalk outside the house.

"He's been in there a long time," said Garrett. "He must have noticed we're not there."

"He should have come out by now," Zach said nervously.

"It's pretty dark in there," said Michael. "What if he fell down the stairs?"

"We better go back in and find him," said Garrett.

The boys went through the creaky gate and up the walk. They crossed the old porch and went into the house.

Inside, Zach yelled, "Andy?"

Upstairs, Andy heard his friend call. Marjory Marbury was still listening to the music. Andy wanted his friends to meet her, so he went to the doorway and called, "Up here."

Garrett, Michael, and Zach climbed the stairs. They found Andy waiting for them in the hall.

"Why are you still in here?" Michael asked.

"We were worried something happened to you," said Garrett.

"I was just showing this lady my iPod," Andy said. "Can you believe she's never heard of an iPod?"

Andy's friends looked puzzled. "What are you talking about?"

"Marjory Marbury." Andy turned to show them the woman in the white dress.

But the woman was gone. Andy's iPod lay on the empty chair. Andy looked around the moonlit room. There was no sign of Marjory Marbury anywhere. He walked over to the chair and picked up the iPod. "She was sitting right here," he said. He looked in the bowl, but it was empty. "She gave me some strange candy from this bowl."

"Very funny, Andy," said Zach. "Marjory Marbury's dead."

"No, she isn't," Andy said. "She was right here."

"No way," said Zach. "She died sixty years ago. And guess how?"

"How?" asked Michael.

"She choked to death on a piece of candy," said Zach. "On Halloween night."

"That's impossible," Andy said. "I was just talking to her. She must have left when you guys came in."

Zach shook his head slowly. "There's only one flight of stairs. We would have seen her."

Andy felt a chill. His friend was right.

"Let's get out of here," said Garrett. "I want to keep on trick-or-treating."

Andy glanced one more time around the room. He didn't understand where Marjory Marbury could have gone. "I'm telling you. She was right there in that chair."

"Sure, Andy," said Zach.

"Whatever you say, Andy," said Garrett.

Andy followed his friends down the stairs and out of the old house.

"Just do us a favor and don't wander off again, OK?" said Michael.

Andy followed his friends down the sidewalk. He knew they'd never believe that Marjory Marbury had been there. For the rest of the night, he stayed close to his friends.

It wasn't until he got home that he put his hand in his jacket pocket. Inside were the rock candy, taffy, and pieces of licorice.

Only a Dream

Samantha Stevens tossed and turned in bed. She was having a bad dream. In the dream, she went into her parents' room. But her parents weren't there. A strange couple was. The woman sitting at the makeup table had blonde hair. Samantha's mother had dark hair. A man sat on the corner of the bed tying his shoes. But the man wasn't Samantha's father.

Samantha woke in the middle of the night and ran crying into her parents' room.

"What's wrong?" Mr. Stevens asked after turning on his reading light.

"I had a bad dream," Samantha cried. She put her arms around her father's neck and hugged him. "I dreamed I went into your room and there were two strange people there."

"It's just your mom and me," her father said.

Samantha's mother turned on her lamp. "Don't be scared," she said.

Samantha saw that it was her parents. She felt better.

"Go back to bed," said Mr. Stevens. "Everything will be OK."

Samantha went back to her room. The light was off. She didn't like to go into her room when it was dark, but she wanted to be brave. She got into bed. Soon she was asleep.

But once again, she had a bad dream. This time, the strange couple was sleeping in her parents' bed. Samantha woke up. Her heart was drumming, and she was breathing fast. The dream felt very real. Samantha didn't care about being brave. For the second time that night, she ran into her parents' bedroom crying. She had to be sure that her parents were really there.

Once again, her parents turned on their lights.

"Did you have another bad dream?" asked her mother.

Samantha nodded. "I dreamed there were two strangers sleeping in your bed," she said.

"That sounds very frightening," said Mr. Stevens. "But now you've come in twice, and who have you found?"

"You and Mom," Samantha answered.

"So if you have that dream again, what will you know?" asked her father.

"That it was only a dream," said Samantha.

"Yes," said Mr. Stevens. "No matter how many times you have that dream, the only people you will find are your mom and me."

This time, Mrs. Stevens brought Samantha back to her room. "I know it's a very scary dream," she said as she tucked her daughter into bed. "But I want you to be a big, brave girl. If you have that dream again and wake up, what should you do?"

"Stay in bed," answered Samantha.

"That's right," said Mrs. Stevens. "Remember, it's only a dream."

She kissed Samantha on the forehead and then left the room.

A few minutes later, Samantha fell asleep. This time, she dreamed it was morning. The strange couple was in her parents' bedroom, making the bed. Samantha woke up. Her heart was beating very hard. Once again, the dream had felt so real. She wanted to jump out of bed to run to her parents' room. Then she remembered what her mother had said about being a big, brave girl. So even though she felt very frightened, Samantha stayed in bed.

It wasn't long before she fell asleep.

This time, she didn't dream about the strangers.

In the morning, Samantha opened her eyes. Her bedroom was filled with sunlight. Samantha was glad the night was over. She jumped out of bed and rushed to her parents' bedroom. She wanted to tell them that she'd stayed in bed even though she had the bad dream again.

Her parents' bed was made, but her parents weren't there. Samantha knew they had already gotten dressed and gone downstairs. She ran down the stairs and into the kitchen.

A man was sitting at the table, reading the newspaper.

A woman was sipping coffee.

They weren't her parents.

They were the strangers Samantha had dreamed about.

Witch Way

"We're going on a campout," said Mr. Sloan. It was Saturday morning. He was standing in the doorway of the TV room. His son, Paul, sat on the couch playing his PSP. Paul's younger sister, Amy, sat on the other end of the couch. She was watching a show on Nickelodeon. They were both in their pajamas.

"Did you hear me?" asked Mr. Sloan.

Neither child answered. Their eyes were glued

to the screens. Mr. Sloan stepped in front of the TV and turned it off. "When I speak to you I expect an answer."

"Hey!" Amy yelled. "It was the middle of a show."

"Why'd you do that?" complained Paul.

"I was talking, but you weren't listening," Mr. Sloan said sternly. "We're going on a campout."

"But it's cold," Amy said.

"It's going to get warmer this afternoon," said Mr. Sloan.

"What if it rains?" asked Paul.

"There's no rain in the forecast," replied his father.

"You always say that the weatherman is wrong," said Paul.

"He's not wrong today. We're leaving in half an hour," said Mr. Sloan. "Get dressed and help me load the car."

Half an hour passed, but Paul and Amy didn't get dressed. Amy spent the time looking at a catalog of dolls' clothes. Paul played with army men in his room. Mr. Sloan got mad. He told Paul that if he didn't get dressed right away he'd lose his allowance for two weeks. And Amy would not be allowed to go to her best friend's birthday party next weekend.

Both kids complained loudly, but they did get dressed. A little while later, they were sitting in the backseat of the car. Their parents sat in the front. Mr. Sloan backed the car out of the driveway. "Here we go!"

"Can we watch videos?" Paul asked.

"Today we're going to be electronics-free," said his mother.

"Boring," Amy grumbled.

Sometime later, Mr. Sloan parked the car in a gravel lot. It was a warm fall day. Gold and red leaves fluttered down from the trees, and the sky was blue.

Mr. Sloan took a deep breath and exhaled. "Doesn't that air smell good?"

Paul and Amy didn't answer. It smelled like plain old air to them.

"Grab your backpacks," said Mr. Sloan. "We'll hike along Witch Way to the campground."

The family began to hike through the woods.

"How much longer?" Amy soon asked.

"A while," said Mr. Sloan.

"My knees hurt," Paul complained.

"Let's see how they feel in a few minutes," said Mrs. Sloan.

"This is boring," said Amy.

Finally, the family stopped for a rest. "Anyone thirsty?" Mr. Sloan asked.

"I'll take a Coke," said Amy.

"All we have is water," said Mr. Sloan.

"I'm hungry," said Paul.

"We have trail mix and fresh carrots and apples," said Mrs. Sloan.

"Can I have a cookie?" asked Amy.

"We didn't bring any sweets," said Mr. Sloan.

"This stinks," Paul grumbled. But he took some trail mix.

While his family rested, Mr. Sloan looked around. He noticed an old cottage in the woods. The windows were broken and the front door was open. A crumbling chimney poked through the sagging roof. Mr. Sloan had hiked Witch Way many times before. He wondered why he'd never noticed the cottage.

The Sloan family started walking again. The hike should have taken an hour and a half. But the children walked slowly and complained often. They made many stops. It was getting dark by the time they reached the campsite. The air felt chilly. The Sloan children sat down on an old log.

"I'm hungry," Paul complained.

"I'm cold," said Amy.

"We'll start a fire and have dinner soon," said Mr. Sloan. "But first, we have to pitch the tent."

"Can't we eat first?" asked Paul.

"It's hard to pitch the tent in the dark," said Mr. Sloan. "If you help with the tent, we can eat sooner."

"I'm too hungry to help," said Paul.

"And I'm too cold," said Amy.

Mr. and Mrs. Sloan pitched the tent by themselves. Then Mr. Sloan went to find wood while Mrs. Sloan prepared dinner. The family sat around the campfire. Mrs. Sloan gave the children metal trail bowls filled with steaming beef stew.

Paul tasted the food and made a face. "This tastes awful!"

Both children refused to take another bite. By now Mr. Sloan was sorry that he'd brought his children on the campout. He decided to tell them a story that might teach them a lesson. "Have you ever heard the story of Hansel and Gretel?" he asked.

The children shook their heads.

"Once upon a time a poor woodcutter lived in the woods with his wife and two children," Mr. Sloan said. "The children's names were Hansel and Gretel."

"Those are weird names," said Amy.

"The woodcutter was very poor," said Mr. Sloan. "He couldn't find enough food for his family. They were slowly starving."

"Like me," grumbled Paul.

"One night, the woodcutter and his wife lay awake in their bed," said Mr. Sloan. "They were too hungry to sleep. His wife said, 'Tomorrow you must take the children deep into the woods and leave them.'

"'But then they will perish,' said the woodcutter.

"'If we don't get rid of them we will all starve,' his wife warned."

"Parents would never do that," said Paul.

"Would they?" asked Amy uncertainly.

"The woodcutter and his wife didn't know that their children were also too hungry to sleep that night," said Mr. Sloan. "They heard what their parents were planning. The next morning, Hansel put a piece of stale bread into his pocket. When the woodcutter led his children into the woods, Hansel left a trail of crumbs."

"So they could find their way back!" Paul realized.

Mr. Sloan nodded. "When they were very deep in the woods, the woodcutter turned to Hansel and Gretel. He had tears in his eyes. He told them to wait while he went to look for a tree to chop down. Then he left."

"What were they wearing?" Amy asked.

"Hansel was wearing lederhosen," said Mrs. Sloan.

"What's that?" asked Paul.

"Leather shorts," said Mrs. Sloan. "And they usually come with leather suspenders."

"What about Gretel?" asked Amy.

"She was wearing a dress and a white head scarf," said Mrs. Sloan.

Mr. Sloan continued the story. "The children waited for their father to return, but he never came back. Finally, Hansel told Gretel it was time to follow the trail of crumbs back home. They started to walk, but the crumbs had disappeared. Hansel heard the birds chirping in the trees. He realized they had eaten the crumbs."

"So the children couldn't find their way home," Amy realized.

"That's right," said Mr. Sloan.

"What did they do?" asked Paul.

"They had to spend the whole night in the dark woods," said Mr. Sloan.

"Where did they sleep?" asked Amy.

"They pushed together some leaves and lay down on them," said Mr. Sloan.

"I couldn't sleep like that," said Paul.

"It was cold and Hansel and Gretel shivered all night," said Mr. Sloan. "They barely slept. The next morning, Hansel and Gretel were hungry and miserable. Suddenly, the scent of gingerbread floated through the air. Gretel and her brother both smelled it."

"I know!" Amy gasped. "The woodcutter's wife made the gingerbread so that her children could follow the smell back home."

Mr. Sloan shook his head slowly. "Hansel and Gretel followed the smell. But it didn't lead them home. It led them to a small cottage in the deepest part of the woods. Only this was no ordinary cottage. It was made of gingerbread, and decorated with gumdrops and candy canes and other candies."

"Sour Power?" Paul asked eagerly, since that was his favorite.

"Maybe," said Mr. Sloan. "The candy was very tempting to the starving boy and girl. Hansel and Gretel were scared because they didn't know whose house it was. But their hunger was so great that they couldn't stop themselves from crawling close and nibbling."

"Something bad is going to happen," said Paul.

Mr. Sloan nodded. "A witch lived in the house. And she caught Hansel and Gretel and ate them."

"Really?" Amy jumped up and ran into her mother's arms. "That's not going to happen to us, is it?" she cried.

"No." Mrs. Sloan hugged her daughter. "And that's not how the story really goes. A witch did live in the house. And she wanted to eat the children. But they were too thin. So she fattened them up with good food. But just when she was ready to eat them, Gretel pushed her into the hot stove. Hansel and Gretel found lots of valuable jewels in the witch's house. They took the jewels home, and after that the woodcutter always had enough money for food."

Paul yawned. "Good story."

The fire had burned down. Red ashes glowed in the dark.

"Time for bed," said Mr. Sloan.

The Sloan family went into their tent. Each of them crawled into a sleeping bag and fell asleep.

Heh! Heh! Heeeehh!

In the middle of the night, an eerie laugh woke all of them.

Heh! Heh! Heeeehh!

"What's that?" Amy gasped.

"Must be an animal," said Mr. Sloan. "Don't worry, it won't bother us. Let's go back to sleep."

But before they could set their heads down, the laugh returned. *Heh! Heh! Heeeehh!*

"That's no animal, Dad," Paul said nervously. "It sounds like a witch's laugh."

"I'm scared!" cried Amy.

Mrs. Sloan reached for her daughter. "Come close," she said. "No one's going to hurt you."

Heh! Heh! Heeeehh!

"Mom!" Amy cried again. Mrs. Sloan hugged her daughter.

Paul was scared. "What's going on, Dad?"

Mr. Sloan's heart was beating hard. He had never

heard that sound in the woods before. "Everything's going to be OK. It has to be some kind of animal."

"Or a witch who wants to eat us," Amy wailed.

Mrs. Sloan held her daughter close. "No one's going to eat you." She looked at her husband in the dark. "Are they?"

"No, of course not," said Mr. Sloan.

With eyes wide open, they all lay in their sleeping bags. Hours passed before anyone in the Sloan family could fall asleep.

In the morning, Paul and Amy wanted to go home right away.

"Why don't we make some breakfast first?" asked Mr. Sloan.

"I don't want breakfast," said Amy. "I just want to go home. I'm never going hiking again."

"I think we should go," Mrs. Sloan agreed.

Amy helped her mother pack up the sleeping bags. Paul helped his father fold the tent.

"See how the work goes faster when everyone helps?" said Mr. Sloan when they were finished.

"Too bad they'll never go on a campout again," said Mrs. Sloan.

"Oh, come on," said Mr. Sloan. "It was just a story."

"What about that weird laughter?" asked Paul.

"Just some animal," Mr. Sloan insisted.

The Sloan family pulled on their backpacks and started down the trail. Paul and Amy walked quickly. They didn't complain or ask to rest.

Suddenly, Mrs. Sloan stopped. "Do you smell that?"

Mr. Sloan and the children took deep sniffs.

"I smell it!" said Amy.

"Me, too," said Paul. "It smells like . . ."

"Gingerbread," said Mrs. Sloan.

The family looked nervously at one another.

"That's weird," said Paul.

"I'm scared," said Amy.

"There's nothing to be afraid of," said Mr. Sloan. "I'm sure it's just a coincidence."

The family continued down the trail. The scent of gingerbread grew stronger and stronger. Mrs. Sloan and the children looked nervously at Mr. Sloan.

"It has to be a coincidence," Mr. Sloan insisted again. But then he stopped. Through the trees, he saw the old cottage with the broken windows. Smoke curled out of the chimney.

"Oh, my gosh!" Amy gasped, and pointed at the front steps of the house.

Lying on the ground were a pair of lederhosen and a white head scarf.

It's Just Wallpaper

"Do you like your new wallpaper?" Mrs. Andersen asked at bedtime on a windy fall night.

Sitting in bed, Courtney Andersen nodded. The old wallpaper had been bright orange, red, and yellow circus scenes. The clowns and lions and dancing bears had scared her. The new wallpaper had green, brown, and blue scenes of children playing in a park. Instead of cages and lion tamers, there were trees and swings.

"I'm glad," said Mrs. Andersen. "You can read for a little while, but lights off at eight thirty."

Courtney picked up her book and began to read. But as soon as her mother left the bedroom, she put the book down and looked at the wallpaper. The boys and girls were riding bicycles, swinging on tree swings, and jumping rope. A boy with brown hair was skateboarding in a playground. Nearby, a pretty blonde girl with a blue ribbon in her hair was riding a bike.

Courtney looked down at her book and began to read again. But then she stopped. Something about the wallpaper bothered her. She looked at it again. Was the boy on the skateboard staring at the pretty girl on the bike? Courtney got on her knees and looked more closely. Was he frowning? Did he look angry?

Courtney got back under the covers and read. Soon Mrs. Andersen knocked on the door and told her to go to sleep. Courtney turned off the light and lay in the dark. In her mind, the brown-haired boy was skating across the playground toward the pretty girl on the bike. The pretty girl didn't see him coming. The brown-haired boy was getting closer and closer.

Suddenly, Courtney felt scared. She jumped out of bed and ran into her parents' room.

Her mother was sitting in bed, reading a book. Mr. Andersen was sitting next to her. He was watching a basketball game on television. Mrs. Andersen lifted her reading glasses and asked, "What's wrong, honey?"

"The boy in the wallpaper," Courtney said. "He's going to hurt the girl on the bike."

Mrs. Andersen turned and gave her husband a look.

Mr. Andersen got out of bed. "Let's see."

In her bedroom, Courtney showed her father the boy on the wallpaper.

"I see what you mean," Mr. Andersen said. "It does seem as if he's looking at the girl on the bike. But has he really gotten closer to her?"

Courtney studied the wallpaper. It did not look like the boy on the skateboard was closer to the girl.

Mr. Andersen smiled. "OK, now turn off the light and go to sleep. It's just wallpaper."

Courtney did as she was told. But as soon as she closed her eyes, she could see the boy skating closer and closer to the girl on the bike. She could even hear the scrape of the skateboard's wheels on the pavement!

Frightened, Courtney jumped out of bed and ran into her parents' room. "I can hear him!" she gasped.

Once again, Mr. Andersen returned with his daughter to her room. They looked at the wallpaper together. "Does he really look closer to her?"

Courtney shook her head.

"It's just your imagination," said Mr. Andersen.

"But I heard him," she said.

Mr. Andersen sat on the corner of her bed and listened. Now he knew what his daughter had heard. "It's the branches scraping against the side of the house in the wind."

Courtney listened. Her father was right. It was just the wind. She felt a little silly. "I'm sorry, Daddy."

"It's OK." Mr. Andersen tucked his daughter into

bed. He kissed her on the forehead. "Now go to sleep. Everything is going to be all right."

"Would you leave the door open a little and the light on in the hall?" Courtney asked.

"Of course." Mr. Andersen left the door open and went back to his bedroom.

Courtney lay in bed and listened to the branches scrape against the house. Soon her eyes closed and she fell asleep.

The light coming through the doorway lit the wallpaper.

Children laughed as they swung on the swings.

Skateboard wheels scraped the pavement.

A pretty blonde girl hummed to herself as she rode her bicycle.

From the shadows came a crash and a girl's cry.

The pretty blonde girl sat on the pavement with tears in her eyes.

Nearby, a skateboard lay upside down.

The boy with the brown hair rode away on her bike.

Don't Sleep Over

Kara Green was mad. "Why do I have to invite Dana Merrill to my sleepover?" she asked her mother.

"Because it's the right thing to do," answered Mrs. Green. "If you want to borrow the Merrills' karaoke machine for your sleepover, then you should invite Dana, too."

Kara balled her hands into fists and frowned. Her

red hair hung down to her shoulders. Her freckles turned pale when she was angry. "Dana Merrill is a loser."

Mrs. Green looked up from her computer. "That's not nice, Kara."

"But it's true!" Kara insisted. "Wait until the other girls find out she's invited. None of them will want to come to my party. My sleepover will be ruined!" Kara blinked hard and made tears come to her eyes.

Mrs. Green lowered her glasses. "Your friends will come to the party because they're your friends," she said calmly.

"Mom, *please* don't make me invite Dana," Kara begged.

Mrs. Green sighed and gazed up at the ceiling. Kara knew that her mother was thinking. She crossed her fingers.

But Mrs. Green looked back at Kara and shook her head. "I'm sorry, Kara. If you want the karaoke machine, you have to invite Dana."

Kara narrowed her eyes and spun around. She stormed out of the room, making sure the door banged loudly behind her. She was already coming up with a plan.

She would invite Dana Merrill to her sleepover. But that didn't mean Dana had to stay.

The night of the sleepover arrived. Kara and her friends carried their sleeping bags downstairs. The basement had soft gray carpeting and a long, comfortable black couch. Mr. Green's exercise bicycle stood in one corner. In another corner were tennis rackets, baseball bats and mitts, skis and boots.

Dana Merrill was the last girl to come down the steps and into the basement. Kara had already shared her plan with her friends. Everyone agreed to ignore Dana. When they sang along with the karaoke machine, Dana didn't get a chance to sing. When they laid out their sleeping bags on the floor, there was no room for Dana's. She had to lay hers down on the other side of the couch.

The girls ignored Dana until she burst into tears and ran upstairs. She begged Mrs. Green to take her home.

Back in the basement, Kara smiled and said, "Good riddance."

Mrs. Green came downstairs to the basement at ten o'clock. She told the girls to turn off the karaoke machine and get into their sleeping bags. Kara could see that her mother was upset that Dana had gone home in tears. But Kara didn't care. It was her mother's fault for insisting that Dana be invited.

The girls crawled into their sleeping bags. Mrs. Green climbed to the top of the stairs and turned off the basement lights. Because it was nighttime outside, the basement was very dark. The girls couldn't see their hands in front of their eyes.

"It's too dark," a girl named Jill whispered nervously.

"Anyone know any scary stories?" whispered a girl named Robyn. She was bigger and stronger than the other girls. Some of them were afraid of her.

"Oh, please don't!" Jill begged. "I'm already scared."

Kara was glad that Jill admitted she was afraid. This was the first time that Kara had spent the night in a basement. She was a little scared, too. But she didn't want to admit it.

Kara's friend Randi had packed a small flashlight. She turned it on. The beam wasn't very strong. But the girls could see one another in the faint light.

"Afraid of the dark, Randi?" Robyn asked in a taunting voice.

"No, I just like to see everyone," Randi answered.

The girls lay in the dim light for a while. They talked about school and clothes and their favorite TV stars. One by one they stopped talking and drifted off into sleep.

Soon the basement was dark and still. The girls slept peacefully in their sleeping bags. Then, suddenly, the karaoke machine went on.

Who's the meanest girl of all?
Is she short or is she tall?

Kara opened her eyes. Randi turned on her little flashlight. The other girls opened their eyes, too.

The red and white lights on the karaoke machine glowed in the dark.

"Who turned it on?" asked Robyn.

"Not me," said Jill.

"Not me," said Randi.

"What about you, Kara?" Robyn asked.

"Not me," said Kara.

"One of you is lying," said Robyn.

Kara got out of her sleeping bag and turned the machine off. Soon the girls were once again asleep.

Who's the meanest girl of all?
Is she short or is she tall?
Why does she make other girls cry?

Kara opened her eyes. Randi turned on her flashlight again. The girls lay in their sleeping bags, staring, wide-eyed in the dim light.

"I thought you turned it off," Robyn said.

Kara looked at the karaoke machine. The lights were on again.

"I did," said Kara.

"You're playing tricks," said Robyn.

"No, I'm not," said Kara.

"Turn it off," said Robyn.

"And this time pull out the plug," added Jill.

Kara got up and did that. Then she got back into her sleeping bag. She had a feeling that someone was playing tricks. But it wasn't her.

Soon the girls were all asleep again. But not for long.

Why does she make other girls cry?
Why does she hurt and why does she lie?

Kara woke up again. She felt groggy.

"What's going on?" Jill asked. She sounded wide-awake and frightened.

Robyn took the flashlight from Randi. She shined it at Kara. "Why didn't you turn it off?" Robyn asked angrily.

The light hurt Kara's eyes. She used her hand to block it. "I did," she said.

"Then why does it keep going back on?" asked Jill.

"You're trying to scare us," Robyn said.

"No, I'm not," said Kara. "I don't know why it keeps going on."

Kara knew her friends wanted her to get out of her sleeping bag and turn off the machine. She just wanted to pull a pillow over her head and go back to sleep. But she dragged herself out of the bag and went to the machine. In the dim glow of Randi's flashlight, she could see that the electric cord was no longer plugged into the wall.

"It's not plugged in," she said.

For a moment, the other girls were silent.

"Does it have batteries?" asked Randi.

"That must be it," Kara said. She looked behind the machine. Sure enough, there was a place for batteries. Kara took out the batteries. The karaoke machine stopped playing and went dark.

Kara sighed with relief and crawled back into her sleeping bag. All she wanted to do was close her eyes and sleep.

Who's the meanest girl of all?
Is she short or is she tall?

Why does she make other girls cry?
Why does she hurt and why does she lie?

The karaoke machine had started playing again.

"What's going on?" Jill gasped in the dark. She sounded like she was going to cry.

Robyn turned on the flashlight. Once again she aimed it at Kara. "I thought you unplugged it and took the batteries out," Robyn said angrily.

"I did," said Kara. She sat up in her sleeping bag. The red and white lights on the karaoke machine glowed. She didn't understand how that was possible.

"I'm tired of your tricks," Robyn said.

"I'm not playing tricks," said Kara.

"I don't believe you," Robyn said.

"Then go see for yourself," said Kara.

Robyn got out of her sleeping bag. She shined the flashlight on the machine. The cord was unplugged and the batteries were out. She pressed the OFF button. The machine kept playing. She turned down the volume. The mean girl song kept going.

"I don't get it," Robyn said.

Kara got out of her sleeping bag. She joined Robyn next to the machine.

"Why does it keep playing that song?" Jill asked.

Robyn made a fist and banged the top of the machine.

> *Who's the meanest girl of all?*
> *Is she short or is she tall?*
> *Why does she make other girls cry?*
> *Why does she hurt and why does she lie?*
> *What did Dana Merrill ever do to you?*

Kara caught her breath and took a step back.

"Oh, my gosh!" Jill cried.

"Why did it say that?" Randi asked.

Kara wondered if Dana had planned this. Did Dana suspect Kara and her friends would be nasty? Did she program the machine to do this if they were mean to her?

> *What did Dana Merrill ever do to you?*

"Make it stop!" Jill gasped.

Thump! Robyn pushed over the machine.

But the machine's lights still glowed. Robyn and Kara bent over the karaoke machine. Robyn shined the flashlight on it and searched for a way to turn it off. Randi got out of her sleeping bag and joined them.

What did Dana Merrill ever do to you?

"It won't turn off," said Randi.

"I want to go home!" Jill cried. She crawled out of her sleeping bag and hurried up the basement stairs.

"Me, too." Randi took the flashlight from Robyn and went up the stairs. Now Kara and Robyn were left in the dark.

What did Dana Merrill ever do to you?

A chill ran up Kara's spine. From the top of the stairs came the sound of a doorknob rattling.

"It's locked!" Jill gasped.

"There's no lock," said Kara. "The door must be stuck."

More rattling sounds came from the top of the stairs.

"It won't open!" Jill cried.

Kara went up the stairs and tried the door. The knob turned, but the door wouldn't open.

"There must be a light," Jill said.

Of course! Kara had forgotten. In the dark, she felt for the light switch and turned it on.

The basement stayed dark. Kara tried the switch again and again.

"The lights won't go on!" Jill wailed.

Kara tried the door again. She pulled as hard as she could, but it wouldn't open.

What did Dana Merrill ever do to you?

The song played over and over. The girls grew more and more frightened.

Kara banged her fists against the basement door. "Mom? Dad?"

"Help!" Jill shouted.

What did Dana Merrill ever do to you?

"Make it stop!" Jill cried.

Randi shined the flashlight back down into the basement. The beam swept past the couch. It stopped on the sports equipment in the corner.

"The bat," said Randi.

Robyn crossed the basement and got the bat. She went back to the karaoke machine.

What did Dana —

Crash! Robyn swung the bat down as hard as she could. The machine stopped playing. At the top of the basement stairs, Kara felt a wave of relief. She tried the doorknob again, but it spun loosely in her hand.

Who's the meanest girl of all?
Is she short or is she tall?

Kara and the other girls twisted their heads. The karaoke machine was lying on the basement floor.

The lights once again glowed, and the sound was as loud as ever.

Crash! Crash! Robyn swung the bat down. She hit the machine again and again. Glass shattered. Pieces of broken plastic banged off the wall.

Why does she make other girls cry?
Why does she hurt and why does she lie?

Crash! Crash! Robyn swung again and again. The broken thing on the floor no longer looked like a karaoke machine. It was just battered, dented pieces.

What did Dana Merrill ever do to you?

"It's haunted!" Randi gasped.

Robyn dropped the bat and ran up the stairs two steps at a time. She pushed past the other girls and banged on the door, screaming, "Help!"

Who's the meanest girl of all?
Is she short or is she tall?

The basement was dark. The batteries in Randi's flashlight had run out. The four girls huddled together at the top of the stairs. They clung to one another and sobbed in fear. Their faces were streaked with tears. Their throats were sore from screaming. Their hands hurt from banging on the basement door.

What did Dana Merrill ever do to you?

Stop! Kara thought miserably. *Please stop!*

Who's the meanest girl of all?

I promise I'll never be mean again, she thought. *Just please stop!*

The doorknob turned and the door opened. The sudden light blinded the girls. Wailing and sobbing, they stumbled into the kitchen, crying for their mothers.

"What on earth happened?" Mrs. Green asked.

The girls' mothers came and took them home. Mrs. Green calmed Kara down. She showed Kara that the basement door worked fine. As soon as you turned the knob, the door opened. The basement light worked, too. Mrs. Green went downstairs to the basement. When she saw the broken karaoke machine, she became upset. Now she would have to buy the Merrills a new one. On the floor she found the CD for the machine. Kara told her to play it so she would hear the song that scared the girls so much.

Mrs. Green played the whole CD.

Twice.

There was no such song.

The Nicest
Babysitter in the World

"Kids, this is Tanya," said Mrs. McPhee. "She'll be your babysitter tonight."

Tanya had long black hair and a warm smile. "Hi, kids. We're going to have a lot of fun."

Derek and Sarah McPhee stared uncertainly at the teenager. She looked and sounded nice, but she was new. And they were always nervous when a new babysitter came.

"You don't have to worry," said Mrs. McPhee.

"Tanya sat for the Smiths last week. Mrs. Smith says she's the nicest babysitter ever."

The McPhees asked Tanya to make sure Derek and Sarah had a good, healthy dinner that night. Mrs. McPhee said the children were only allowed to watch one hour of TV. Then they went out.

"So what would you like to do first?" asked Tanya after Mr. and Mrs. McPhee left.

"Play Candy Land," said Sarah.

"I love that game," said Tanya.

They played Candy Land. Derek thought Tanya was lots of fun. But once when Derek looked at her, Tanya looked old. Her skin looked wrinkled, her nose hooked, and a hairy mole grew from her chin. Derek rubbed his eyes, and Tanya looked like a teenager again.

"It's time for dinner," Tanya said when they finished playing Candy Land. "What would you like to eat?"

Derek and Sarah knew they were supposed to have a "good, healthy dinner." But those dinners were always boring.

"I wish we could have ice cream and cookies," said Sarah.

"Good idea," said Tanya.

Derek and Sarah stared at each other in surprise.

After a dinner of ice cream and cookies, Tanya said. "What do you want to do now?"

"Can we watch TV?" asked Derek.

"Sure," said the babysitter.

After. they'd watched TV for an hour, the McPhee kids looked at Tanya. "Do we have to turn it off?" asked Derek.

Tanya shook her head. "You can watch as much as you like."

Derek and Sarah grinned. Their mother was right. Tanya was the nicest babysitter in the world!

The McPhee kids watched all their favorite shows. After a while Tanya said, "Is there anyone in the neighborhood you don't like?"

"Why do you want to know?" asked Derek.

"Oh, I don't know," said Tanya. "It just seems like everyone has someone they don't like." Then she smiled. For a second, it looked to Sarah like some of Tanya's teeth were missing. The other teeth looked crooked and yellow. Sarah blinked. When she looked again, all of Tanya's teeth were straight and white.

"Mom says we're not supposed to say bad things about people," said Sarah.

"I know," said Tanya. "And you're not supposed to have cookies and ice cream for dinner. And you're not supposed to watch all the TV you want. But isn't it fun?"

Derek and Sarah nodded.

"Talking about people you don't like is fun, too," said Tanya.

Derek wasn't sure. But Tanya seemed so nice, and they were having lots of fun. So maybe she was right.

"There's a boy down the street named Billy Thomas," Derek said. "Sometimes he throws rocks at us."

"Really?" Tanya said.

"Yes," said Sarah. "And he once kicked our dog. And another time, he pushed over my bike and broke one of the pedals."

"That's not nice," said Tanya.

"And he says bad things, too," said Derek.

"That's terrible," said Tanya. "If you could get back at him, what would you do?"

Derek and Sarah shared a look. It was as if Tanya had read their minds. They'd always wanted to get back at Billy.

"I'd push *his* bike down," said Sarah.

"Not me," said Derek. "I'd hit him as hard as I could on the arm."

"I'd throw a rock at him," said Sarah.

"Me, too," said Derek.

"And it would feel good, right?" Tanya said. "After all the mean things he's done to you."

Derek nodded. It would feel good. But thinking about it made him feel bad. "Our parents say it's wrong to hurt people."

"Does Billy Thomas think it's wrong?" Tanya asked.

Derek and Sarah shook their heads.

"Then maybe sometimes it's wrong," said Tanya. "But sometimes it's not."

Tanya let them stay up past their bedtimes. When it was finally time to go to bed, she said they didn't have to brush their teeth. Tanya tucked Sarah into bed and then came into Derek's room. She sat on the edge of Derek's bed.

"Did you have fun tonight?" she asked.

Derek nodded. "I wish you could always be our babysitter."

"I wish I could, too," said Tanya. "But I have to go away tomorrow, and I don't know when I'll be back."

Derek frowned.

Tanya reached into her pocket. "Would you like to have a picture to remember me?"

"Yes," said Derek.

Tanya gave him a picture of herself. Derek put it on the night table beside his bed.

The next morning, Mr. and Mrs. McPhee couldn't understand why their children slept so late. Mrs. McPhee called them for breakfast. Derek and Sarah came down and sat at the kitchen table. Derek felt groggy and slow. Sarah had a stomachache.

The McPhee children didn't touch the pancakes their mother had made. Derek had no appetite. He wished he could put his head down on the table and go back to sleep. Sarah looked pale and sat with her arms folded across her stomach.

"What's wrong?" Mrs. McPhee asked. "Why aren't you hungry?"

Derek and Sarah didn't answer.

"Did something happen last night?" Mrs. McPhee asked.

Derek and Sarah shared a look. They both shook their heads. They didn't want to tell on Tanya.

"I don't understand why you're acting like this," said Mrs. McPhee. "Tanya said you were both perfect angels."

Derek slid down in his chair. He had not been a perfect angel. He'd broken the rules last night. It was fun to do the things he wasn't supposed to do. But this morning, he felt bad. Maybe it wasn't always good to get what you wished for.

The phone rang and Mrs. McPhee answered it. "Hello? Oh, hi, Linda. What? Oh, that's terrible!"

Mrs. McPhee looked very upset. She hung up the phone and shook her head sadly.

"What's wrong, Mom?" Derek asked.

"That was Billy's mother," Mrs. McPhee said. "The most terrible thing happened. Billy got up early this morning and went for a bike ride."

Sarah and Derek shared a nervous look.

"Did someone push him off his bike?" Sarah asked.

"No," said Mrs. McPhee. "It's even worse. Someone threw a rock at him. He fell off his bike and knocked out both front teeth."

Sarah and Derek stared at each other with wide eyes. But neither said a word.

Later in the morning, Derek went back to his room. He tried to play with his Legos, but he couldn't stop thinking about the night before. Both he and Sarah had said they wanted to throw a rock at Billy.

Then Derek remembered the picture on his night table. He got up to look at it. In the picture, Tanya smiled at him with her straight white teeth. But in his hand, the picture began to change. Tanya's nose grew long and hooked. Her skin became wrinkled, and a hairy mole grew from her chin. Her teeth became crooked and yellow.

The next thing Derek knew, he was staring at a witch.